*k*New

the Chapbook

TL Sanders

FLYING KETCHUP PRESS ®
KANSAS CITY, MISSOURI

Dear Public Libraries,

You dedicate so much to us; thus, I dedicate such work to you.

Some of the following poems have previously appeared in kNew: the Screenplay
Flying Ketchup Press. 2019. Thank you to FringeFest KC and Fountainverse
Poetry Festival which gave audience to live performance and this publication!

cONTENTs

aCKNOWLEDGMENTs

Thank you, Lyric Opera of Kansas City
for granting me the *opera*tunity of a lifetime by making me a pearl
diver during your staging of Bizet's The Pearl Fishers. The cast was
filled with such superlative talent. Because of that experience, I
gained enhanced and heightened acuity for sound, movement,
and delivery. Thank you to Flying Ketchup Press for their work in
making this book possible. "This fire ignited inside me lights a way
for my passion to stop hiding . . . It's exciting." And thank you to
Paper Birch Landing Contemporary Art Gallery for making this
chapbook and screenplay come to life through the opportunity
granted to me as 2019 Poet in Residence.

BECOMING

ᵂe Cover the Cover

We've read the works the GREATS created
And lived and loved and died and hated
Our lives' reflection—frustrated, relieved
Because in the characters ourselves we see

Now, let's believe it's meant to be
We cover the cover of our stories
We write them down from head to tail
We tell our tales both bad and well

We author books, our former dreams
From which we wake and take the themes
A phrase, one word to three—four
More pages enslaved 'til we restore
Ourselves we see penned deep in color

For it's our names written on the covers

*M*omentum

Most moments it spends
With her with him with them
And then it hits the brick the wall

And rolls downhill from here to there
Their body is minding its flesh is flushed
Straight up against momentum's touch
Is scattered and shattered
absorbed
contained

Only to be released again

FOR LOVE

If not for love
Then for what?

For Love fills up those empty cups
Love holds old souls

The Lull
The Like
The Lust
For Love
   to live
     then Love
       must love

If not for love
Then for what?

Senses

So stressed
Uncomfortably forced to wake up
So annoyed
Sit up
So tired
Stand up
So weak

Partly, wanting just to sleep
Fully, knowing I need my dreams
I
Get up
Go get
The things
For me
Are not in this bed

−Kalique Sanders

*O*r Not . . . To Be

I don't feel like being here
Being here keeps me locked away from being
Being there is where I would like to be

To be or not to be?
Not to be; I'd like not to be
I'd like not to be, but I didn't have a choice

A choice was already made for me
My choice already made me
Made me see my
Wrists was slit with slits
Shallow slits sit still, still staring at my holey soul
Holey . . . an adverb describing reverb
having heard Holy Hell's dead headless horseman holler how
horrible a human

I was born to be

To be or not to be?
Was Hamlet's soliloquy
He chose to be him; Let to be him
Let me
not to be
Not to be my feelings

Hurt

My feelings
form and forget and forget to form the future
The Future forgets to form Sutures' hands that help heal slits,
Hands that help heal and slit ice packed hits,

Ice packs hit cracked back bones broken by word sticks and word
stones that they said would never hurt

Word sticks and word stones that they said would never hurt
They said they would
not ever hurt.
They lied
So did I
I Lied, too,
to my face

My face
lies on my pillowcase breathing in compromise
In compromise I decide
I decide to live

I

decide
to live
To live or not to live is not a question
To live is not a question; it's a choice
A choice that I chose to make

I chose to make it
To make it

I choose to make it
To
make
it
not about feelings
It's not about feeling shallow slits sitting still
still staring at my once holey soul

My once holey soul had a win
A win adds a "W"
A "W" changed my old, ~~w~~hole soul to my whole soul
My whole soul is no longer holey

My whole soul
is wholly whole
And
I
am here
I
am whole
I
am me
I
am free
I
Choose "To Be"
I choose to be more

Now it's your turn
It's your turn

It's your turn to choose

A Change of Mind

I was blind
she was blind

Closed our eyes,
intertwined
wanted more than we could give

You Only Live Once was how we lived

I fell in lust
wanted love
I had no glove
So guess what

A surprise, a baby life-love unborn
I can't lie; we thought we might
just abort

We changed our minds

So then Nine
months
later,
I'm Handcuffed to child support

I fell in lust
wanted love
I had no glove
So guess what

Our relationship sunk
It didn't work
We broke up

My car broke down
I couldn't work

We fought in court
I lost in court
I lost my kid
I lost all hope
I lost my mind
I lost all drive

I fell in loss,
and despair drove me to the place where I didn't care
I couldn't care
for myself
I daily questioned why I was here;

Even though I had no
Used to be
There was one reason:
My child was needing me.
At least that what I told myself
This drove me to drive myself out of depression.

I wrote down my feelings and reread my reflections
Rear viewer's discretion was advised.
I was reminded of that surprise,
a baby life-love unborn lived

I can't lie; I thought I might stay ripped and torn

I changed my mind
And guess what

Nine
Months
Later, after sitting in court,
I stood up and repaid all back child support
And then some more

I gave of money and my heart
For my little girl,
I made fatherhood a work of art

Plus, found a job
Bought a car
Stayed auto driven on a mission promised myself
Not to be missing another moment of her life

I used to think that I would die blind
I changed my mind

Now, I live with eyes opened wide!

Polished Poet

This piece of art - Language Art - is for all of us
from the famous to the infamous
artists devoted to go their hardest
no matter how hard

It is my kiss blew
to you whoever wrote, glued, or drew
emotional emojis eventual
overflow overflows oxytocin birthing birth-
an ocean of extra strength
Ibuprofen dopamine doctor's notes

I hope you note
your poems, pictures, paintings, and photos
are the consoling strongholds
healing cracking parts and broken hearts of the hopeless

In exchange for pain your word less
writings are inciting peaceful rioting
widening the true meanings of what hope is
I
quote this
from my boldest piece on golden canvas
for the Beethovens interwoven with the writers

Who
Can

You can
paint framed pictures
without cans of paint or picture frames

My camera aims toward the trap singing,

tap dancing,
archiTech N9ne-type writers who weld . . .
Weld wild things wilder than the wildest dreams

I'm
talking to you
writers who
forge . . .
Forge forks in the road to allow the not yet writer
alternate routes without . . . Knives
cutting them off
putting words in their mouths

To the painter whose purpose is out
standing, planning
fate's great adventure
determined to add venture
past the signs that say
DO
NOT
ENTER
and pounce on the path unpaved
revising the road's name from, "Not Taken"
to Shakespeare's Lane
saying, All the world's a stage

I want to remain
that writer

A poet who performs off script
freestyling on topic
to the point that he has polished
each piece
like Beyoncé be
slaying
each beat
she and Jay-Z
erit

DJ Jazzy Jeff
Fresh Princess
Destiny's Child
I snap on beat

Let me be—
that writer on a mic strapped stage,
in them dim lit streets,
or in the front of a class on the edge of my seat
with a pen and a pad putting life to a page
making paper want to read

ADAPTING

Are Violets Blue and Roses Red?

It has been said that Roses are red and Violets are blue

Unless

The Violets are violent
So violets are red
Like all of the time
They wish roses were dying
Dead in their beds
Pushing up daisies
Yeah, violets are crazy
And acting all shady

I dunno maybe
I can say safely
Violets are red
Because violets are angry

And so roses are blue
You would be too
If violets aimed violence
And pistils at you
Roses are red?
That ain't all true
Instead of the red
Rose is actually blue

Being exceedingly sad
Yet playing it cool
Not real sure what to do
Or how to elude ultraviolet pursuit
Or to quiet the tyrant
Or calm down the climate

Or pilot this crisis
These violets is ISIS

Killing its kindness and niceness
The rose grows to icy
Grows poison like ivy
Grows tired of stymie
So no go on hiding

Thorns come out fighting
Swoosh, Just Do it—Nike

Other flowers will likely
Say—roses are feisty
Forgetting—when it politely
Begged—violets to Spike Lee

Do the right thang
Did violets change?

The colors they once were
Are now rearranged
To this day,
Roses violate violets
So fate makes
A stigma of hate
The symbols and pigments
Of petals re-written
Now roses are red
Red is indignantly ignorant

While violets are brilliant
Stole the script
Flip it

Then for an instant
Pretending religion
New image same mission

The Grinch's Christmas
White Lily my witness
When Rose was listless
Violet did finish
the ones on its hitlist

Painting roses malicious

It shall ever be written
That just like the violets
The "Roses are Red"
And just like we read
What we already knew,
"Violets are Blue"
And roses are too

#Realtalk

Real talk today
means US, the human race
speaking
with the meanest
hate,
setting backstabbing mouth traps on greenest stage
watering reasons and ways
we will never be great

Real talk
is when they
"Keep it 100 Percent"
then say something plotting against
the one person
we're supposed to love

Let's let go of
false facts
find truth
redefine that
"real talk"
should be defined as - some folk just for fun break word
Bonds to hate on
you and her and him

To condemn

The definition of "real"
Talk from fake folks whose main aim
is to use your name in a lame joke
I believe the game is
to roast
us placing blame on

us putting shame on
us pulling fame from
us
All because of applause

That ain't probable cause
Y'all
we chose those
infamous friends
bragging 'bout boatloads of dough
you know, Big Benjamins, Dead Presidents
and C-notes

but think though
they got jokes
Coach, they can't quote "Money is talk"
when
their talk is cheap 'cause
they stay broke in hoping
you don't focus on those cash flow holes in their pockets
dropping lies
you're witnessing with your own two sockets

If you're listening
then Listen
and
LIVE
doing the opposite of letting
Them lead

You
urgently need to
start stopping it
Real talk

I mean
it's obscene seeing you demeaning the truth
when you know it's not a surprise you can walk in a booth

disguised a regular Joe
but burst out a hero
who personifies superman's alter ego
as described by Quentin Tarantino
in his film, *Kill Bill*, he reveals "Superman"
didn't BECOME Superman

Superman was BORN Superman
when Superman wakes up in the morning,
he is Super.
Man,
some friend's real talk is stupid.
man,
let's use x-ray vision to peer in
peers' opinion
visually hearing how

We allow Shallow Hal villain minions to make us miss our mission
Must I mention even how Superman caged himself in
the invention of

Clark Kent...?
Clark Can't
And he didn't cause Clark is a figment
of an outstanding man's imagination to blend in
with regular humans who struggle to stand

But then again, I've been there, too
After
walking a mile in used shoes
trying to fit
in wearing the fool's costume
wondering when my parent was coming home
and
if he did, would he pay rent
or were we gone
was the fight gonna be on
were the lights gonna be on

or the heat or the water or food gonna be on
our table
so we could eat
so we could sleep
so we could
sew the holes in our souls'
train wrecking all hope of dancing
dreams once bright now
dimming lights
of right and wrong these nights are long and days
are pawned

Life's kryptonite changes crypt to night
you pick a *Bic*¬¬—a knife
the razor to end your life
turning your wrist upright
holding your fist real tight
straining a vein to slice
hoping tonight it might just work
taking your life
and
the hurt you
can't help yourself
at first
you wondered the worst

What
if
you
fail? You're adding a pill not wanting to feel
Failure
already felt when you tried something else
alone in that field where you wept
sidestepped death
got up and left, unhealed

Concealed and carry
the risk

you watch your wrist
for fear of killing time
you time your kill

#realtalk

Over time
it
over kills you
over fill
the bottle
your belly
the barrel
but barely

You overfill the steel chamber and clips
and still
you over feel your spirit refuses to slip
so you skip quit
till your body and soul split . . . the deal's real a
bet
a Russian Rou-lets a bullet to your head
but fate called and said "There's a reason you're not dead!"

Remember you're the super kid
What does a bullet prove to the person who is bulletproof?

Suicide's no sacrifice

#realtalk
is when the tiger in your eyes forces you to realize
that stack of sticks and stones has always been a sack of lies
You survive
Real talk

It's when you brace for broken bones
but your last nerve has gone numb
from

A fighting spirit forgetting permitting repeated demise
Repeated demise lies in words
Repeat It
"Demise
Lies
In words"

Spoken limitations have taken tokens from your skillset
over the years you've let
others' opinions of you
steal that skillset

Even still that
mindset
falsifies logic
making you think you can't get the thing in your dreams
yet
you've already got it

Bet

Real talk
Is courageous fear
It's Being present when no one cares you're here
It's
Speaking up when no one dares to hear
it's
the difference between the victor and the victim

I was almost one . . . a victim
with them
those who almost won
their battle against the system
but they didn't
and now they're gone
I guess statistics
Just picked them to be victims of a world beyond
this

Earth
A birth into death
In the same moment,
Love,
laughter, life, all left
memories we won't let go of

Real talk
is the real thought
the real chalk outline
lining the body of your buddy
laying in a bloody crime scene

Yes.
Pain is blinding

No.
you can't cave

You're mining
in this
dark cave
you are
finding shining diamonds in the rough
stop hiding in the rough
start reminding
you
yourself
are beautiful, intelligent, thoughtful and tough. Thus
you clean up the crime scene

Real talk is
it's a crime seeing and not believing in your being
that you are born more than capable of being
more
than just real talk

I*n* TIME

Fear leads life
Life dreads death
Death seeks truth in Time

No matter the year, the season, the month or moment
Most fears are distant whispers
screaming reasons life is to run out light

A heaviness - A scared to death

Time ticks till one's breath slips away
No care for race or age or sex
Some say it's wrong, but Time is right.

Yeah, Time is always right on time
So, is it time?

Fear, life, death, seek, truth, it is time

Wednesday, Mourning - *Oklahoma City 1995*

Wednesday morning before 9:02 AM
A sleepy-eyed five-year ½ kissed her daddy good-bye, fully
expecting to give him the other half later

Wednesday morning before 9:02 AM
A mother hugged her mother for a moment longer, as if to say,
"Mommy, your strength makes me stronger."

Wednesday morning
before
9:01 ticked toward 9:02
In sum, Love granted both breathtaking and heartbreaking
moments
As Grandfather Time foretold the beginnings and endings of some
stories to come

Then   When
9:02 came   Crashing in through the window
Pain   Palmed
Promises

Shattered both glass and hopes
of a ½ kiss, she'd never give
of next memories, they'd never live
For a girl would wait fatherless
A mother would mother motherless
'Cause a son, who shined sunless,
caused darkest to rain on hundreds

And So I Shall Love Because

You will not make me hate my flag.
A devotion to the union dates back to before All Americans were included
In the writs wrote to depict its constitution.

You will not make me hate my flag.
Today, some go assuming
When I am choosing to take a stand or a knee
Or I choose when to speak or to pledge or to sing
Then my action must be
Terrorism.

You will not make me hate

My flag lived long on the days when Americans were slain at the hands of other Americans.
It was under its gaze both the Civil War took place and this place took Civil Rights
It was wrong White Knights of the Ku Klux Klan, the Blue Klux Klan, and the Rouge Klux Klan
Cut ties and tied ropes, copped a dog and a fire hose to wet red white shirts of those
Blue blooded Americans
Did the Devil's work right after they left the church and witnessing
A sour lynching is best served cold post a hot meal and sweet dessert
Was death deserved?

Naw bruh!
You will not make me hate

My flag flew to fights making the Counterfeits take flight and fall
Mouth full of the dust they were forced bite
Must be *dusty armies like*
The Confederate
You will not make me hate
Our flag and our stars and our stripes
Flies high and soars low paving ways and humble roads
Holding close the chief goals to gather together, to unfold
Both US history and migrant stories untold.
We know that the flag stands with liberty and justice for one nation undivided
Hence it's in the name of our country
The America's *States United.*

I've decided to love
Because
You will not make me hate *my flag*

TRUTH

A hollow cave deep within its feelings
hinge in time

It's time
to reach for humble hope, a noble rope
that binds boundless vines

A hallowed cry - a swear by life's divine
to search and weep and seek to be the try
Yet never finds

A never mind can cave the chest
of us all and cause the called to call the quits

This never mind collapses fallen tears
They drip
atop the treasured chest that hides
within a hollow cave
just behind a second time

DECIDING

Enjoy these poems by T.L. Sanders from *kNew: The Poetic Screenplay*...a biopic moment at the heart of open mic night in the famous Blue Room in Kansas City's Jazz District. These poems are part of a story T.L. Sanders weaves around Dr. J. Dean, a quiet family man who leaves his job at Penn State to fly to Kansas City to mourn the death of a father he hardly knew. There, in the old neighborhood where his father Terry Dean performed, The Blue Room holds just another stage where anyone can spit some lyrics. But this night, a new vision awakes when a community grieves a prodigal father. Something new emerges in the hearts of those willing to speak their truth . . . each voice melds into a new revelation about this family's past.

A Son's Watch, A Father's Walk (Dave Dean)

i remember
watching my dad walk
walk from some unknown room, holding
his Kangol Cap, the hat with the kangaroo.

this dude looked extra cool
in his fresh pressed suit and shiny shoes
on his feet they sat at a slew.

yeah, he seemed slightly slew footed.
that's when feet point at ten and two
like strangers confused as to their next move
so they choose to separate and go separate ways
unlike his feet, mine were straight.

but i changed
my gait to glide wide like that guy's.
i would mimic how
his right foot would slide
with the luck of a hockey puck
passing the buck to the left one,
a scuffed-up stone skipping on ice
broken by a shock wave
waiting to rock my world twice
as my father waived his rights
while forgetting to wave *Goodbye*.

i remember
watching my dad walk
walk right out of my life

i followed that walk with my eyes
blurry and burning

until all i saw
was
silent
sound waves crashing beneath
deleted footprints that washed away
the soles of my feet.

my soul,
had feet that walked away
the same way
leaving me on my knees
to plead and to pray
as only the misunderstood could.

i guess God guessed i would
share dad's drift walk and dare
to bare his missed fate.

oh, by the way,
my dad served time
for a life of Crime
that did not pay
and that unknown room
from whence he came
was a holding cell which lay
behind a courtroom gate.

what can i say,
Papa was a rolling stone.
Wherever he lay his hat was his home.

my papa,
was a rolling stone
a rolling stone with a chip
and i was the chip of the old block
the old cell block.

i remember

watching my dad walk
then watching the clock,
wanting that father time
would tell him that
i'm the missing piece
who was missing peace
like my father,
time ran out on me.

painfully, watching my dad's Watch
i wore on my wrist
and it was with that Watch
that dad watched me waste time.

watching and feeling the clock's tock tick
with my pulse which
fell when he left
Each footprint hurt the most
Pain
i'll never forget
Each
click of his heel matched the tick
of my Watch
i watched
Each
click of his heel matched the tick
of my heart
until
his heel click changed to the click
of a gun clip and POP!

my pops shot
the tock of my heart broke and stopped
only to say, *Nope* when i wished it to heal.

i remember watching my dad walk

until time froze my thoughts

to prove neither my Watch
nor my eyes were waterproof
so i fell through thin ice
like life's levee just let me break
down every ounce of hope held
in a jammed mirror never found.

i was a river dam
the damned river wanted to drown
me
collapsing my knees
flooding my bodily soul was so weak.

Yet . . .

It wouldn't break.
It thunder-clapped back at everything
throwing shade on my unmade grave
I
gave up giving up
I started getting up
from the depths of the dumps
I started living up to my fate
as a chip off the old block
This chip became the rock,
a 373 Carat diamond shard
easily formed
from a life that was so hard

So, hardships with this hard knock life made me
Captain of the Guard and King to follow my lead
Surviving past the day daddy decided to leave

Miss me with the mess
Statistics believe folks like me won't succeed
and won't go no further than life with no father
May not make sense but my senses grew stronger
than my circumstances

As to distance
I went even farther than far
Fought harder than hard
For even if I fall in quicksand
and I wanna call it quits
Man, I yell, *Hell naw*
Then still stand
Taller than tall
To evolve

My soul holds my breath
as I fall down below sea level
It is only then when eyes see level
and fly toward the sky
and the glide will be level ground
On which I found:
In order to rise up,
one must first fall down

half of SHE (Hope Dean)

SHE
was spit in the face. SHE was smacked in the face.
SHE was spit, slapped, smacked, and kicked in the face

Her stepdad beat her back into a corner
when SHE turned to face the corner,
he beat her back
This was back when SHE was eight, to be exact,
on her birth date
no, no candles
or no cake

Her birthday wish was to trade
the corner for a coroner
to trade
the corner for a coroner

SHE
whispered this wish 'til sleep mixed
his spit with her tears
Even her tears had tears
that died that day
died, dried up on her swelled-up face

As SHE lay, in that curled up place
SHE dreamed a dream
of her real dad, her father,
who was locked away

And SHE wished real bad
real dad was back
so absentee dad would kick that . . .

As for he, this replacement pappy
happily turned on SHE
saying, *So sad your dad burned on you, Boo-Hoo-Hoo*
Then he
pulled out a CD, a burned one, too
Playing a mixed tape of Timberland and Timberlake
Cry me a River" with "It's too late
to Apologize" this guy would die
before he'd repent; so as to not let this moment slip, he didn't
relent

He sent his message was verbal violent
fake playing air violin
he began, *Your old, man . . . jail birdie*
Even when that fool flew free,
dummy deadbeat didn't dare beat his rap sheet
I'm MC Hammer. He can't touch me

The con man comedian started laughing
while cracking jokes and joints
jamming stick sharp points
that poke and play sick games with pain,
to hurt her heart
to drown away her soul
so, step down dad prolonged the grasp and hold

Her gasps for air no one could hear
so, step down dad's reply was, *No*
one cares
Followed by I told you

So . . .
Every
Single
Day
SHE counted every day
one
by one

Finally, the day had come

Celebrating

Twenty-one and single
Goes out to mingle
Meets a merry magic man. He's a match.
They marry and just like that,
the match catches fire
Unjust, just like her fathers both
the one SHE had and the one SHE didn't

Now is just like then
SHE's living in a time,
SHE can't even fidget. For it
is more like dying
SHE can't even envision
a relationship without hitting
One without crying
One with no hurting

Not so controlling

No con trolling, scolding,
holding his hand around her throat. Choking
the life out of
HOPE
had her vision
blurred by two black eyes
He told her a couple of times,
A woman's place is in the kitchen

Where she's sitting
and SHE's mourning, morning sickness
reminiscing
on things real dad should had done
But did he? No, he didn't
Good riddance. Forget him

And to the dude who fathered her this infant,
SHE won't be missing his tripping
on second time forgiveness
SHE tried to give a thousand times
he justified the why
he did this
with threats to end his
Mini-me must try to master
and survive its first trimester

Alabaster midget bastard
Embryo pro-life disaster
Followed fast and followed faster
Like a raven on a lake
Litigious
Religious
Roe v. Wade Supreme Court Case
Gave a grave gift
On her birthday
Baked bakers men burned patty cakes
Cupped hands to face
Spit and spew hate
Like SHE ain't
There's no serenade, no hope, no faith
For HOPE is made to celebrate with just her fate

On this date SHE's twenty-eight
Aunt Flo is fate
Where is God's grace?
For Heaven's sakes, SHE is HOPE and lonely

Her son is the only man who understands
The problem is he's unborn
He is barely a baby

SHE's pregnant
SHE can't—but maybe . . . irrelevant
The pregnancy test read a red plus

Thus, SHE guesses SHE'll wait a couple months

And then SHE'll go to the clinic

The day delivers Death's panic
SHE steers the wheel
SHE's frantic

SHE steels her will
SWAL-
lows the pill. Tries to lie still.
And still, tries to lie
This baby is not alive.
So how can he die?

More panic!
SHE can't conceive he's going to be
an aborted baby

and then it–The Forceps

Reach in,
Grab him
And then
It
Is over

He's dead;

_Spitting Image (Dr. James Dean)

I hold a photo of my father.
We have twin eyes. Twin smiles. Twin laughs.
We were twins, separated at birth.
My birth.

This photo that I hold holds my stare
And I
Can't help but to compare
My father's picture to the reflections in the mirrors

Only to remember
Feeling rejection as the symptom to
Our Father son-system was
An absenteeism
Kind of had him but I didn't
That dude liked to go to prison
This forced a long distance
Relationship with my dad

And I had a realistic fiction
Backed by black boy statistics
Fact is Crack was his business
Smack injections was his mistress

He our Mister fallen hero
Had an evil alter ego
So our bellows barely echoed like one yelling
Through a pillow
Case
That fellow chased
The killer's cape to collapse the pain into his veins
The villain's name
Is Heroin

It's harrowing
His heroine was Heroin

Let that sink in

I inherited some substitute Samaritans

I'm not trashing the compassion that they had
But a back-up dad is not a real comparison

Sadly
I was not the only one
See
My dad had a pair of sons
And
A daughter who he didn't dare to daddy

Siblings
I'm sorry for our loss
Since this
Donor
Like many other fathers who
Couldn't live further from the truth
Decided to up and move to be the farthest father
From you
And me

We
Had non-existent re-la-tion-ship
Yep he
Left us the permission
To depend on government assistance
And still
No food would we be getting
So we would steal
Not to be greedy
Sneaking food soon led to eating
Daily hunger fed our pleading

Homeless Shelters willing feeding
Us
Little bastards
We were needing
Thus, the cycle kept repeating

'Cause a conscious had insisted
Violent crimes he kept committing
The court system quit acquitting
Sending dad to the detention
Meaning, I had a visit him in prison
Relationship

As a child this made me sad
Seeing my friends had had their dads
Go figure
Movie stars and friends' fathers were
The father figures in that path
Paving ways to add the stats

When I stack the good and bad
Times
The times I needed Dad
Then
I count the countless tears
Filled with joy and pain and fears,
Equals
The reasons why
Double struggle toils and troubles
Force a flex of that spirit muscle
Underneath debris and rubble

I rise and shine
My light shines light on wrongs
To show they really were right
For me to be the man I'm meant to be

And man

I'm meant to be
This father figure
For my midget mirrored image

Maybe some of y'all remember
How your father really didn't

Or you're the father who really isn't
Active in your child's existence

We must choose to be persistent
And in action ask forgiveness
While
Knowing our repentance
Will
Affect how our descendants
Decide to be the kind of parents
Repudiating disappearance

It should be apparent
For females
This means to mommy
And us dudes
We're due to daddy
Just as I didn't ask my donor
My own kiddos didn't ask me
To be a parent who represents
Cemented-strong relationships
Should be healthy
Never sick

So to remedy the symptoms
Of failed father-kid systems
It is actually rather simple:
Be the parent who always picks
To commit for permanence.

Sounds Good Smells Bad (Mrs. Holeman)

I knew the whispers before
I heard them

They sounded good
Smelled bad

Sometimes bad smells serve purpose
So I closed my nose to hold focus

I needed to be all ears
Good morning, Beautiful

$\mathcal{A}$udience of One (Mr. Holeman)

Since my audible love is meant for an audience of one,
I connect vocal cords to this corded mic,
allowing my mouth to voice what my soul knows . . .
knew . . .
I and It love endless with a part of us that lived long
before anyone even ever breathed a breath.

Upon the day when the last blood leaves my lungs
may my first, best heart dialect be left for you.

Plus, a fat insurance check, too.

And, if or when I have to go . . .
Please. Know
that the smallest sum of you adds more to my life than numbers
can do in all of math
In fact my stat's level reads the same from front to back before
the first Anthropomorphic Contract was signed on Rhind
papyrus.

A pure love like the devil fell for evil
But Good that's equal to the Genesis prequel
When God rose us from dust.
From clean dirt He formed her—

My love,
When I go I will miss the curve
of your eyes, hips, butt, lips;
those nice thick thighs.

I keep a dime all of the time
as a subtle way to remind me of your fine
wine glass is a tall drink of water.
I will miss your mind—the way you think.

Our conversations bring me to the brink of completion. Period, and so on!

The day I die will be too soon.
For I shall regret my throat lacked the know-how
to pronounce my vow above the clouds
to shout it, scream it, sing love loud.

My soul and I shall disavowal
this apprehension didn't teach me how
to truly echo passion's growl–
my lull, my like, my lust, my yearn, my joy, my peace of

You are the reason I want to sleep
so to see you in my dreams
the why I can't wait to wake
next to the real thing.

You are my why I don't need to breathe.

See, I wish to leave all of the oxygen you need.

And times when we do not share the same room
I abate my breath–to save air.
As your groom of thirty-three years,
I can safely say you've never taken my breath away
I give you it and me, freely–
Endless with a part reserved especially for an audience of one.

PO-etry (Dr. James Dean)

First of all, I must thank the Lord that I was lower than poor

I was my poverty

It didn't help that I was raised on a road called Roach Street
Ironically, we shared our home with one roach
Times infinity
Usually these roommates would sneak to school and be
The reasons friends would make fun
Of that destined situation

My students don't think I see the problems they are
Hating to live
Waiting to leave
Please, I saw when I was awake
I see in my sleep

I repeat—I grew up PO-
You see, my best way out was PO-etry

I was the child of a missing dad and gone dope fiend
Being both my parents
A felon father fleeing freedom for prison
And street prescription
Given to treat a mental illness condition
Of my mother
I love her
Her struggle was real
See, she was the only one
I could depend on
But still, since she couldn't stop it
I was adopted at age eleven
A former slave to my friend's father's idea of heaven

My friend's father's idea of heaven was boys—Abandoned
So he misled and let them
Live with him and then he did
UNSPEAKABLES
In the sight of his son
So I never spoke for I was unable to speak
of those nights to no one
But God
I prayed in broken English and fits of sobs
God answered.
He took the job.

I
am
you

See, I grew up
I got out
I found deep down in me was preparation to meet each need

By reminding those fighting internal wars blindly
Instead of breathing quietly
Shout
For the mouth without Hope's voice
Falling
Through the floor without floor joists
Holding up
The past without pro choice
Without a mom
Without a dad
Without true friends not mad when asked for food

This guy was you
Needing others not think that your smell is a joke
To understand it is not your fault that you smell like smoke
Even though, you now are a house burnt down
By the kinds of people who point with Steeples at your sin
When they themselves own the same means to the same end

But live lies to pretend like they have never ever sinned
Or have ever NEVER been
Broken
Hungry
Homeless
Lonely
Hoping for just once
Only if only
The ground beneath us would quit moaning and groaning
Making miracles atone for this endless mourning

It's morning outside
Yesterday the sky cried
Today its rainbow bright
Blends in for you are the blue in the bend

It's morning outside
Again
You're mourning inside
Again

Your struggle within is forcing you
To embrace death's ideology
'Cause the afterlife has got to be better
Than a Murphy's Law apology
Especially when written in a last rites letter, right?
Write, No, in the deepest, brightest parts of your soul
Suicide mustn't be an option

When facing a problem
The First Step is stopping
Stop letting where you are at
Be the mindset that determines how far you can get

Yeah, you've been cut plus stabbed in the back
But use a suture
Fix your eyes on a time in the future
Wrap your hands round the straps of your boots

Or your bow aimed by you
A well-trained archer after success a target much larger
You are not a problem
You are THEE
Problem Solver

The Second Step
Remember where you were
Experience has knit the sack, your quiver
So set a goal, get your arrow, let it go
And when you grow
Tell them, _Oh . . . I understand_
Your story
Might be the sword in her hand
Tell him, _You are me._
Tell of how you used to be the epitome of POV-erty
But now you know the best way out undoubtedly is PO-etry

*O*xygen (James)

The true hero is you
who struggle with addiction

For today is not the day you give in
To what you want more than oxygen
And even though you love breathing,
You choose to hold your breath despite
The pain that you've felt
Or you feel
Will
feel

In spite of the cards you've been Dealt
Are dealt
Or
The deal that you made with your child's other parent,
Which turned out to be a facade
Faking false odd visions of a hope that you had.
Now you are looking at the dope that you have
In your hands those prescription meds
In your head old descriptions and
New wishing
Man, with just one hit, a stiff sniff
You'll forget

With just one pill and quick prayer to repent
This pain too shall pass . . . giving you release
But You
Hold your breath
Knowing release won't last
Won't last as long as the longing you've had to have back
Your daughter and son
Who's been gone for far too long

So you hold on to
Holding hope
Empowering the truth to manifest
The words to say no to dope
And in that moment, you
Breathe through the torment

Yeah, you let your arteries and capillaries
Carry oxygen-rich, courageous fear
Diminishing the lingering years
Of your addiction convictions
With each breath you force
Your body to reject the notion
That your addiction is needed
And you believe it

Your thoughts spell words
Words
That speak life's song of triumph
Your words endorse actions
Actions
That remodel decrepit mansions
Your actions auction habits
Habits
That win over your life as an addict
Your habits create character

Ladies,
You stare at her in the mirror
And in the dark
When you can't see
Her internal beauty is revealed even clearer

Now my brothas, I know you've been told
your contents within were meant to explode
Well it did —blew the lid
And you didn't die

which is why the content of character is what you're judged by

Ladies and gentlemen,
say hello to this new self
Who left addicted behind
'Cause my people,
You're too strong for an addiction
To be beating your behinds

Keep in mind
Your vision.
The main mission to be more like
Jesus less like Judas
To be like useful not like useless
To do this
You wear a sterling silver necklace
A reminder less of a reckless past
And more of God's forgiveness
That lasts passed eternity

You are determined to be
In your children's children's children's lives
Forming positive legacies
That appreciate nothing less than quality excellence
It is this type of character that paves new roads
In those old neighborhoods
Where our mothers and sisters and daughters are called hoes.

Were called hoes
Now our women know
They have the power to change
What society says they are destined to be

And with this knowledge,
you say with words out loud
THIS ADDICTION WON'T GET THE BEST OF ME

Your breathing

Is intentional like your thoughts
Your body
Holds your mouth accountable when it talks
And through all hurts,
You let those who set out to repudiate your self-worth
Walk Away
'Cause you know that today is not the day that you give in
To what you want more than oxygen

✒nd Forever After (Brotha Man)

Well, considering the given predicament,
I present this BlackLivesMatter sign as a present
sent to be opened in silence

Listen.
Sankofa eyelids allow us to live colorblind and
move forward while truly being reminded
our job, as a people, is defined in acts of kindness and in how
we're reviving life to dying conversations

Think of applications when places ask what one's race is
He could mark other
Ideally, the hue of the applicant applies less
to levels of melanin pigment
and more toward the kind of person
by which one wishes to be depicted

The hint is the kind of man
The tint is the hue,
man is meant to mix and blend
with hues of men regardless our skin
We didn't pick it

It's no picnic
We know
picket signs guide blind mankind
to future contracts we both co-sign
We're buying the whole goldmine outlined in light
where white whisks all colors to illuminate the night
helping us see tangible pieces of Peace

Gently open our eyelids and read with deeper belief
The black lives matter sign had to happen

My Dear Applicants,
Black represents all the colors combined
as one
when it comes to pigments.
Comprehend that
I'm not trying to rain on your parade or your protest.

Although the question that remains is,
Have we noticed the aftereffect of rain brings a rainbow?
Can you see our pots of gold through your soul's window?
Pain and hate, they have to go
Leaving Love of Laughter to be mastered
Making racist cancers and natural disasters
two wrongs that turn us to the road of right answers

Yesterday, today, and forever after

𝒜 **Destiny Destined to Be** (Destiny Jae)

This Christmas gift wrapped is you
You're taken aback
'Cause there are two
Options
    One: You could run
Purposefully leaving open the door
Just in case you wanted to take a field trip to nostalgia

To spy on that memory,
The moment you refused the deed to your true destiny
But don't fret 'cause what's left
You see, is still loved

Option 2:
You
Wait
Watch
Cautiously touch twin's mirror

You hope that this part of you stays
Brave
Honest
Strong
Confident
Heaven sent
Fire—Your eyes not sad not timid
This instant
Intelligence your posture attests expresses no limit
In you . . .

This you
is a fighter
True Colors shining through

are Brighter

Think the sun

Now go brightest
As bright as the brightest
Star discovered by man, like Sirius

Yeah . . . Serious. The brightest star in night's dark sky is named
Sirius
Greek for scorching
Go brighter
Torching
Go brighter
Touching something that makes daylight seem like night
Like the lightest light lifting limitation allowing liberty to linger
Linking the larks lullaby to the lives before your eyes

Don't ask, Why?
Just Go
Brighter
No might or wait let me think

No! Don't think for one wink
that you depict anything which personifies weak
Know!
That you already are the brightest star that man has never met
And introduce yourself to yourself
Loose yourself from steel shackles that
start to starve who
You are
shaped to their demands

The real crime is they don't mind their blindness
Thus, they fail to see difference
between iron ore and diamonds

See, they don't get that

one needs a diamond pickaxe
to extract iron ore
For
diamonds are more than ore
and you are more than diamonds

That reflection that hides beside your door
no longer dies outside anymore
It lives
inside you
Denying every attempt not to allow your true colors to shine
through
You
Are more than iron ore and diamonds

More

The limited mind of science

More

Than even the discovery of giants

You are greater
Infinity
Times two, at least

So people can't mine you!
Not a single piece of that which defines who
What
When
Where
How and the other questions on these tons of quests that you
will at best outlast
for you
are timeless . . .

Remember

In this world of shackles,
it's your job to seek out and find you.

Look at Option 1
But choose Option 2

Shock and Awe (Poet in Red)

If I were to tell my secrets
my deep secrets that hide behind
My deeper secrets
That hide behind my deepest secrets

I fear that I would see regrets

If I were to tell how I really feel
To reveal . . .

I'm **Sorry that I'm So Sorry** (Terry Dean)

Heavenly Father,
I plead forgiveness for not taking care of
the children you have given us.

Now, to my daughter and sons

I am so sorry I have the habit of being absent.
I am an addict.
But a day hasn't passed when I didn't think of you.
And to this day I still do
Remind my mind I haven't
Been a daddy who's worth having.
While other dads were Happy Birthday buying,
Christmas wrapping,
You lived my lies in hades
Blindly waiting and self-saving
Maybe thinking that your daddy hated all of his babies.

The truth is I love you kids.
I'm sorry I didn't give a kiss.
I'm sorry that the only gift.
I gave was life and that I missed.

I am so sorry I am sitting here
With these friends
In this Motel Styx
Swearing a quick river dip
Will grant me life by crucifix.

I am Sorry it makes little sense
That even though it's drugs I do
It's always you I choose to pick.

(God, I pray they're seeing this.)

I guess what I am trying to say is
If I had a dying wish
I'd wish that you did know
You're my purpose to persist.
I exist
For you four
Are the parts of my heart that is whole.
You're my Hope, atria, septum, and ventricles.
You're my bright souls on dark cold, frozen rainy days
When I pay for dope only to know
I'm both the buyer and the slave,
A hero in heroin's cave.
No chains and yet I stay
Unchanged.

Please forgive the unforgivable.

I and it—pitiful.
The way I lived—criminal.
How much I love
You never know
Because my hiding
Love on islands
Busy fighting to stay quiet
So my feelings could not show.

For fear of reaping what I've sown
I wrote this note in crisis mode.
I'm writing wrongs to right my wrongs.
Ready to die to live to learn
If you will give or I may earn
A chance for freedom—My parole.
Hearing you all care to care
Will be earth, water, fresh air
To make me see me sober
Belief that I must leave

This here.

This life for me
Has been a crystal meth stained staircase.
I hate that I love
The splinters and the tacks
And the clinging to the railings
And the feeling like I'm falling
So I'm crawling on these steps.
And I'm feeling my skin crawling
So I'm clawing at myself.

And still, nothing seems to help
Me from building bridges I keep burning
Reaching landings but preferring
Climbing back to smack,
Returning back where I'm at
To who I am—condemned
A boarded-up crack house
With no doors
Methadone for most floors
Covering the window pane,
In the place where curtains hang,
Is kitchen cooked crack cocaine
Combined with shots of heroin
Was the things that got me through
Or so I thought.

But now I think I can't make it
Through if I don't have you four
So once more, I am so sorry
That as your daddy I am so sorry.

No matter what happens,
Daddy loves you all

I see you   Always

aBOUT THE AUTHOr

Did you know that *kNew* is an award-winning solo show as well as a poetic screen play? The performance of this groundbreaking project was awarded *Producer's Pick Award* during the 2019 KC Fringe Festival.

POET t.l. sanders, AKA *Àtwist*– whether at a performing arts center, a theater, a classroom, or a conference– will illuminate, educate, inspire, provoke and surprise. To Sanders, language arts, poetry is a way up and a way out. His vast experiences as a performer, speaker, event emcee, teacher, curriculum writer, and mentor, make his work meaningful to a wide variety of audiences. To book him for your event, contact him at www.poettlsanders.com.

fLYING kETCHUP pRESS...
to discover and develop new voices in poetry, drama, fiction and non-fiction with a special emphasis in new short stories. We are a publisher made by and for creatives in the Heartland. Our dream is to salvage lost treasure troves of written and illustrated work- to create worlds of wonder and delight; to share stories. Maybe yours. Find us at www.flyingketchuppress.com or on Submittable.

dESIGN NOTEs

The font selected for this book is Adelle in honor of its clean, simple lines, breathability and its history of being built by an unlikely pairing that began a new thing – much like this book! Veronika Burian and José Scaglione created this font together launching the independent type foundry called *TypeTogether* in 2006. Cover Design by Carie Sanders of Creative Souls Design.